Christmas on the Black Meadow

Chris Lambert

**Illustrated by
Andy Paciorek
and
Nigel Wilson**

First published in Great Britain in 2016 by Exiled
Publishing, South Street Arts Centre, 21 South
Street, Reading, RG1 4QU

A CIP catalogue record for this book is available
from the British Library

ISBN-13: 978-1539767244
ISBN-10: 1539767248

blackmeadowtales.blogspot.com
lambertthewriter.blogspot.co.uk
exiledpublications.blogspot.co.uk
soullesscentral.blogspot.com

Other Works by Chris Lambert
Published by Exiled
Tales from the Black Meadow
Songs from the Black Meadow
Some Words with a Mummy
The Comic Mystery Plays (2017)

Published by Wyrd Harvest Press
Wyrd Kalendar (2017)

Published by Verse
"First Step" in Dead Files IV
"The Treehouse" and "Dead Man on the Moor" in Dead Files V

Published by CFZ
"Pilot" and "The Catalogue" in Tales of the Damned

Published by The Ghastling
The Most Precious Possession
The Patient

Published by Stagescripts
The Simple Process of Alchemy
Ugga – A play about a boy with a paper bag on his head
Ship of Fools
Loving Chopin

For
Robert Henderson
and
Robert Addie

All profits from the sale of this book go
to Worldwide Cancer Research.

Contents

List of Illustrations

11

12

Introduction

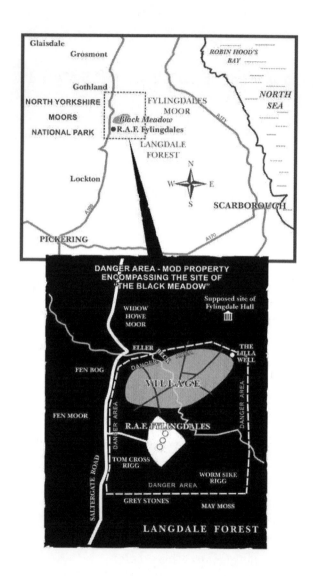

Introduction

Professor Roger Mullins, a folklorist and researcher from the University of York, spent several Christmases on the North York Moors in the 1960s.

He was researching the area known as the Black Meadow[1] as well as the various customs and tales about the area.

It was in the Christmas of 1967 when he was staying at The Plough[2] in Sleights that he met Francis Tresham[3], a local farmer who told him of a strange experience he had involving, what is now commonly known as, a *land sphere* at Christmas time. Several other locals were keen to tell their Yuletide tales. He

---

[1] Much has already been said about this area and you can find further information in *Tales from the Black Meadow* (book Published by Exiled; album by The Soulless Party available on Bandcamp), *Songs from the Black Meadow* (available from Mega Dodo) and *The Brightwater Archive*.

[2] *"A warm welcome awaits you at The Plough Inn in Sleights. Situated at the top of the village under Blue Bank, The Plough offers spectacular views across the Esk Valley."* (*Taken from www.ploughinnsleights.co.uk*)

[3] See *The Black Star* (page 97) for further details. Roger conducted a detailed interview with Francis and his wife in 1968.

15

heard a new tale about a Meadow Hag[4] as well as interesting titbits about blackberry farming. One of the locals told him that the best Christmas tale would be found at Old St. Stephen's Church[5] near Robin Hood's Bay. Roger went armed with a camera, notepad and pen to record one of the strangest and most heart-warming tales to come out of the Black Meadow.[6]

As you sit down in your armchair by a roaring fire, with a glass of warm blackberry wine[7], to read this Christmas tome, be prepared to be charmed and horrified in equal measure. Prepare to have your cockles warmed too.

---

[4] For more information about Meadow Hags see *Tales from the Black Meadow* and *The Black Meadow Archive*. See also *The Meadow Tree* (page 65)

[5] *"Well worth a visit, the interior of Old St Stephen's Church has not been changed since it was rebuilt on an existing site in 1822. Come and see the box pews (last repainted in 1917 - and why do half the pews face backwards?), a West Gallery and a three-decker pulpit."* (Taken from *www.oldststephens.rhbay.co.uk*)

[6] See *A Black Meadow Christmas* (page 19).

[7] Blackberry wine is a traditional drink on the Black Meadow, due to the proliferation of bramble and blackberry that grows there.

If you venture into the snow on the Black Meadow this Christmas, avoid the mist, for strange things dwell there.

A Black Meadow Christmas

Old St Stephen's Church, Robin Hood's Bay

Introduction

(The following is taken from the notes of Roger Mullins – Originally published in "Undiscovered Heresies" in 1975 (three years after he disappeared). Reprinted with the kind permission of the Mullins estate.)

"I often visit the churches on the outskirts of Black Meadow and one had a somewhat curious tradition. Old St. Stephen's Church in Robin Hood's Bay - which closed in the late 19th century - is famous for its display of Maiden's Garlands, created to mark the passing of virginal girls. On the advice of a customer at The Plough in Sleights I visited the church to gather some possible Yuletide lore. One of the curators of this abandoned church showed me an ancient photo of a very different curiosity.

The picture showed the porch of the church. Placed in the porch were two very different Christmas scenes. On the left was the traditional nativity; a baby in the manger with a smiling Mary and Joseph, Ox, Ass and all the trimmings. The other scene on the right of the door was very different.

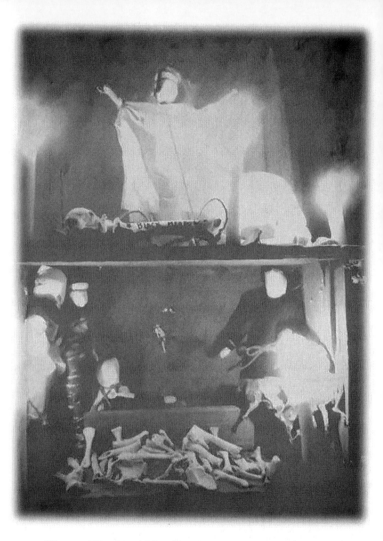

The Black Meadow Nativity Scene (photograph taken in the late 19th Century).
On the top of the barn you can see the Lady of Mist flanked by a desiccated rat and a skull. In front of her is a bone with "Black Meadow" inscribed upon it. Inside the box from left to right are James and Maria, the old man in his coffin and the priest.

I asked the curator and he was very keen to outline the reasons behind this most peculiar display. This is outlined in a transcript of his explanation below."

"You've not seen anything like it have you? Sometimes the Christian Church took on pagan practices and made them their own, perhaps adding their own little spin.

Corn rigs at Harvest festival time and all the gathered offerings of food echo the old pagan offerings to the Celtic gods...

...Easter eggs have their links to fertility gods....

Even the giving and receiving of gifts at Christmas has its roots in Saturnalia.

Religions don't simply replace, that wouldn't work. So instead they cherry pick appropriate rituals and beliefs and adapt them, making the new religion more palatable.

Detail from Black Meadow Nativity scene.

Note the priest and the desiccated rats. These are substitutes for the sheep of the tale. Note also the use of bones instead of straw.

However this was something quite different from that usual process of borrowing and adaptation. This was a very local custom and something rather unique.

This inversion of the nativity must have started many centuries after Christianity was first introduced on these shores. Some said it was an expansion of the Christian tradition, whilst others said it was an abomination. For many years the local priests allowed it to satisfy local superstition, sometimes they even accommodated it into their preaching. However the Archbishop of York was visiting one Christmas and took a great dislike to what he saw. He said the church was tainted. Some say that is the real reason the place closed."

The following folk tale explains the strange nativity scene that Roger Mullins witnessed.

A Black Meadow Christmas

And it came to pass that a mist fell across the land, one Christmas Eve, many years ago. It did not come from the sea but from the Black Meadow. People were very afraid as the mist licked at the borders of Robin Hood's Bay. Very near the gates of this church a very old man (some say that he was over a century in age) walked out of the fog accompanied by a young man and a young woman. Following this strange trio were fifty head of sheep. There was a tremendous noise behind them as a large group of villagers broke through the fog. They were chanting merrily and banging drums. Great big warm smiles lit up their faces. They all followed the old man to the church, respectfully matching his sedentary pace.

The people of Robin Hood's Bay were making their way to midnight mass on the cold Christmas Eve and saw this odd crowd approaching. A whisper went through the congregation that these folk were from the Black Meadow – a place steeped in dark mystery for centuries. The congregation shuffled inside and shut the door behind them.

As the priest said his opening prayer to his nervous parishioners there was a rapping at the door. The priest gave his "Amen" and strode down the aisle. The young man and woman stood outside. The young man smiled. "Can we come inside? My name is James and this is my sister Maria. As you can see my father is very old. He would seek to celebrate with you on this cold winter's night. This may be his last chance to take mass."

The priest looked at the crowd of revellers, the sheep, the son, the daughter and the wizened old man. He looked back at his quarter-full church, at the frightened faces of his parishioners. He shared their fear.

"We have no room," he said, turning back.

"But we have been to two other churches and they have said the same," James pleaded.

The priest looked guilty and something stirred in his breast. "We have no room here but you can shelter in the adjoining barn and celebrate there."

James thanked the priest and turned to the revellers. The priest shut the door and returned to his congregation.

The old man, James and Maria, the flock of sheep and the revellers walked to the barn. They hung their lamps from the rafters, huddled together for warmth and sang a song of mist and bramble.

And while they sang a mist rose above the barn and began to spread throughout the village.

Some shepherds were tending a few mangy ewes in the hills above the town. Their sheep were the last remaining of a flock that had been decimated by disease and cold over the last year. The shepherds looked in wonder at the mist spreading in the land below. The mist seemed to twist and knot and curl and turn itself into fabulous shapes, one of which looked like a beautiful maid. She seemed to stroll across the top of the cloud as though it were a fine carpet of wool. She waved at the shepherds. The fog rolled towards them carrying her swiftly into their midst. The shepherds looked in wonder at this magnificent sight. She reached out and touched the chief shepherd on the cheek with her fog fingers. He marvelled at the touch; so soft, so tangible and yet he could still see the stars through her skin.

"Greetings," she sang. "Tonight I bring sad tidings of great joy. For on this night the father of all will meet his end. Come and pay homage to him. Join in his final dance."

The shepherds looked at one another before running with the maid down to the barn. They were met by a joyous sight. An old man sitting, surrounded by the people he loved. The songs being sung were loud and glorious, rattling the rafters with their volume.

The noise had interrupted the service. The lacklustre singing of the old carols was no match for this celebration of a life soon to end. The priest and his congregation stormed to the barn, flung open the doors - ready to throw out these interlopers - but found themselves immediately beguiled by the revellers' joy.

James approached the priest and shook him warmly by the hand.

"Welcome. Thank you for coming."

The priest smiled weakly and wished God's blessings on them.

The revellers shouted a "Hurrah" at this and sang another song with a chorus so catchy that the congregation found themselves joining in. James turned to the priest.

"My father does not have long to live. It is his time. May we bury him here? Do you have a coffin we may use?"

One of the congregation raised his hand, identifying himself as a carpenter and told them that he did indeed have a coffin that would suit the height and build of the old man. The carpenter and the priest left the barn, returning half an hour later with the coffin. They opened it up and placed it in the centre of the barn on the floor.

Maria took her father by the hand and led him to the coffin. He climbed inside, commenting on how comfortable it was.

An old widow ran forward from the crowd of parishioners and placed her shawl in the coffin for him to sit on. He thanked her graciously and lowered himself down. The old man looked around the barn, a beaming smile wrinkling his face. He waved the shepherds over.

"Take my flock," he said. "I have no need of them and they will bring you great prosperity."

At another wave of his hand the sheep trotted over and joined the shepherds who were filled with gratitude.

He then turned to the old woman.

"Thank you for the shawl, it shall be a great comfort to me as I lie in the peaceful dark." He reached into his jacket pocket and pulled out a small bottle. "Take this perfume. It will delight your senses and make you feel young again."

The old woman curtsied and took the bottle graciously. It is said that she lived for a good many more decades and always seemed to have a young gentleman on her arm.

The old man gestured for the carpenter to walk to him.

"Take this incense. I have never had use for it but I hear it is worth a fortune. I know that it will pay for this very comfortable coffin and for a thousand others like it."

Finally he turned to the priest. James walked forward carrying a small but weighty sack that jingled as he moved.

"Take this gold," the old man said. "From this day forth welcome all into your church, old and young, poor and rich, different and similar. Let this gold pay for clothing, shelter and food for any wayward travellers who pass through your walls."

The priest nodded. Then he stopped and asked the old man, "Why did you come here?"

"To die."

"Why do you wish to die?"

"I do not wish it. All things die. All things stop and do not continue. But we must look after the living. While we live that is all. Remember the living, bury the dead, let souls fly where they will."

48

He lay down and closed his eyes.

His breathing slowed.

The rise and fall of his chest came to an end.

He smiled.

James and Maria stood at his head.

The shepherds and their new flock gathered at his feet.

The priest, the carpenter and the old woman stood by the door holding their gifts of gold, incense and perfume.

The lady of the mist floated above the barn whilst crowds of revellers from the Black Meadow and the congregation of St Stephen's Church sang songs together into the night.

Traditional Gifts from the Black Meadow

Figure 1 - A Bramble Cradle

What would you buy your child for Christmas if you lived on the Black Meadow?

You will be aware, of course, that the majority of people who inhabited the villages in the area were of little means. This meant that a trip to the shops to buy the latest steam train set, weeping tin soldier or exciting board game for aspiring grocers would be beyond the average inhabitant of the Black Meadow. That is not to say that children went without at Yuletide, far from it.

Roger Mullins discovered several items that would have pleased a child on that most blessed of mornings.

The first of these is the Bramble Cradle (*fig. 1*). The Bramble Cradle is a perfect gift for a child from the Black Meadow. The father of the household would create a wonderful cradle for his child's doll that the rest of the family would festoon with fresh bramble pulled from the mist-covered fields. This toy cradle was, as everyone knows, a re-creation of an actual bramble cradle. To prepare their children for the hardships of blackberry farming, parents would add bramble to

53

the bedding of an infant in order that their soft skin would become used to the incessant scratches and cuts associated with that most cruel of plants. Eventually a child would become almost immune to the perils of the bramble; their skin hard and calloused.

It is often said that older children, who had gone through this process in their infancy, would find it hard to fall asleep without a sprig of blackberry on their pillow or a bramble branch in their nightshirt pocket. For a child, the gift of a bramble cradle for their doll would allow them to practise this ritual in preparation for their own offspring in later life.

Sir Stanley Coulton discovered the following popular lullaby that gives an insight into this ancient tradition. Imagine a mother singing this to her children as they settle down for the night in their uncomfortable bed, blackberry leaves and bramble thorns scratching at their skin. Imagine too, those children, warbling out that same rhyme to their own dolls resting so softly in their bramble cradles.

Lie so still
My little one
Do not turn your head
The pillow soft
The sheets so white
Will turn to darkest red

Turn your head
My little one
Do not be afraid
The bramble fierce
Will seem more soft
Than sheets on which you're laid

Sleep so soft
My little one
With skin so bonny fair
The thorn and spike
Are cotton clouds
A'drifting in the air

When you wake
My little one
You'll swim the fields in joy
For bramble cuts
Are sweet enough
For ev'ry girl and boy

Figure 2 - A Grumbling Rod

What do you give a young blackberry farming lad?

Grumbling Rods were commonly seen carried by adolescent boys around harvest time. Decorated with spirals and stripes, varnished and polished to a bright sheen, before being topped with a crown of tangled bramble, these were items of great value to a young man entering the turbulent waters of puberty.

At the harvest festival the boys would stand in a circle, Grumbling Rods held above their heads, chanting:

"Come come blackberry come
Join our song."

Maidens from the village would then crawl under the legs of the boys singing:

"The blackberry comes
To join your song."

The maids would stand together in the centre of the circle, backs to the boys. They would hold hands with each other and dance a slow step anticlockwise, singing:

57

*"From the Bramble fair
Through the Bramble air,
Snare our Bramble hair."*

The boys would lower their Grumbling Rods so that the bramble crowns were level with the heads of the girls. They would then dance a slow step clockwise, chanting:

*"From the Bramble
To the Grumble,
Let us Tumble
To the Bramble"*

The boys would then try to reach the maiden's heads with the bramble crowns. The aim would be for the maidens' hair to get caught in the bramble on the end of the Grumbling Rod. If a boy snagged a maiden (or caused her to "*grumble*" – which they invariably did when bramble tangled with their hair) then she was his for the harvest dance.

Needless to say boys were very protective of their Grumbling Rods, as a "*well-kept Grumble*" was said to be the perfect snare to capture a good wife.

Sir Stanley Coulton discovered this charming rhyme about the Grumbling Rod dance in 1874. The chorus and verse are said to overlap, to mimic the call and answer of the girls and boys in the grumbling dance.

Dancing two steps
Stepping one dance
Left to right
Right to left

Must you grumble
Sweet maid so fair?
For the bramble
In your sweet hair
Is as a jewelléd crown.

Dancing two steps
Stepping one dance
Left to right
Right to left

Can we tumble
Sweet maid so fair?
For the bramble
That we share
Will be our eiderdown.

Figure 3 - A Thorner's Helm (drawn by Roger Mullins) –
Picture donated by the Mullins' estate.

Perhaps the most prized of all potential yuletide gifts is the Thorner's Helm.

This beautiful leather hat is riddled with specially sewn holes for bramble to thread through. This, like the bramble cradle, is used to harden a child's skin against the cruel thorns of the bramble. However it is also thought to have certain mystical uses. Thorner's Helms are passed down from parents to children and shared amongst the siblings. They are created from a highly preserved leather that can last for generations. They are never washed, so the sweat and, vitally, the blood of generations mingles and mixes inside. A Thorner's Helm, therefore, is considered to contain the essence of a family. This, in the right hands, can be used to bless and preserve a family line, conversely it can also be used to curse and damn a bloodline. For this reason they are closely guarded by families.

A new Thorner's Helm would be a real rarity as they are so seldom made. A leatherworker of great skill would be called upon to make one and at some cost. To prepare the leather it is soaked for two months in a mix of blackberry cordial, boiled urine and a cup of mingled blood (taken from all the living members of a family). It is dried and stretched before being cut and sewn into the finished helm.

When it is handed over to the family by the leatherworker at Yuletide, a *Hatting Ritual* takes place. In this ritual the leatherworker knocks on the door nine times, saying with each knock:

"Once for the father
Twice for the mother
Thrice for the sister
Fourth for the brother
Fifth for the old
Sixth for the young
Seventh for the berry
Eighth for the Lord
Ninth for the maker a'knocking at your door"

The father opens the door, inviting the leatherworker inside. The leatherworker is offered a goblet of hot blackberry wine which he has to drink down in one gulp (if he does not he is offered another). The leatherworker holds the Thorner's Helm above his head and sings:

"Let the thorns scratch
Let the blood fall
Let the skin heal
Let the bramble call."

Each member of the family takes a length of bramble in their hands. The father takes the Thorner's Helm from the leatherworker, threading his length of bramble through the holes in the leather before passing it on to his wife, who, in turn, passes it to her children. As the Thorner's Helm is threaded the family repeat the leatherworker's song:

"Let the thorns scratch
Let the blood fall
Let the skin heal
Let the bramble call."

The Thorner's helm is ready. The youngest child wears it first, all the family singing out, for one final time:

"Let the thorns scratch
Let the blood fall
Let the skin heal
Let the bramble call."

The Meadow Tree

The Meadow Tree

The following tale is one of the latest that Roger Mullins found. It is believed to be set in the late 1920s or early 1930s. Considering it was so modern he was surprised that it had gathered considerable word of mouth and he found varying versions of it on his travels. For those familiar with the Black Meadow there are some elements that tread shared ground with other folk tales from the area. The fact that they do this shows the power that Black Meadow phenomena has over the local populace.

"Beware of pedlars selling wares with a mist behind them." – Traditional North York Moors saying

The young man's mother had always regaled him with cautionary tales about the mist, which, like any sensible son, he ignored utterly. The ramblings of a silly old woman were not to be taken seriously. The lights of Robin Hood's Bay faded behind him as he drove his noisy open-top automobile sputtering onto the moors. As tarmac road turned to mud

67

track the dormant bramble rose on either side. A beautiful white mist sat in the twisted branches in little wisps of spectral cotton candy.

The road widened ahead. The young man slowed his car as he approached the rickety old stall. Beautifully made multi-coloured paper chains hung from bowed wooden railings. No sign hung above the wares instead wreaths of holly adorned the shack. Sturdy white candles carved with snowflakes and stars sat upon the dirty worktop. The young man swung open the car door, stepping out into the bitter cold. He studied the stall, his pockets jingling with coins.

His first Christmas at his new home would be one to make his mother proud. She had not wanted him to leave her side but the time had come. His job paid handsomely and so now he could pay his silly but darling old mother for all her pains and care. The first thing he would do was to treat her to a wonderful Christmas. Cook a fat goose for her, lavish her with gifts and dazzle her with a houseful of decorations so splendid that she might even be stunned into silence.

The shops in the town sold the usual frills but it was not enough, it would not do. She would know where he got it all, she knew all the shopkeepers, knew their stock, nothing surprised her. After trawling through several dull establishments, turning his nose up at far too many lacklustre wares, he found himself standing despondent in the main street. A gentleman with collars up and a hat pulled down over his brow beckoned with crooked fingers.

"Not good enough, eh?"

The young man looked baffled at the stranger's words.

"I've seen you in and out of every little shop upon this street. Going in with such anticipation and coming out in such gloom."

The young man nodded. The stranger tapped the side of his nose, leaning close to whisper in his ear.

"There is a place you could try. It is a little out of the way but you should find what you are looking for. It is all very unique and magical my son, perfect for that first Christmas in which you want to make an impression."

So, armed with directions, the young man found himself on this old dirt road, miles from home. Hemmed in by dry bramble and heather, with a cold fog all around, looking upon the most splendid Christmas fare he had ever seen. The lights, the baubles, the wrapping, the mangers and the trees. God bless that stranger! The trees, so lush, so full, so tall, sitting proud within their pots. He started to make some choices about what he could purchase and hoped that he had enough money to pay for the many items that caught his greedy eye. He looked about for the keeper of the store but could see no one. The lanterns were lit and burning bright. He called out a "Halloo" but heard no reply. He considered that this may be a stall run on trust in which money was left for products taken. He had heard of such places, but looking at the quality of the goods, he considered it unlikely that anyone would leave these wares unattended. Still the night was growing old and he had no intention of staying on the moors, in this mist, any longer than was necessary. He walked over to one of the carved candles and reached out for it. As his fingers began to trace the intricate etchings upon its wax skin, a hand shot out from the dark and grabbed his wrist. He gave a girlish yelp and turned to look at his assailant.

A small wizened ancient lady in a dark coat and hood gazed up into his face. She grinned at him with crooked brown teeth. Her face was so wrinkled it resembled a dehydrated peach he had once found behind the dresser. She gave a little chuckle and released her grip.

"She's sorry. She didn't mean to startle him," she croaked.

The young man tried to smile but found that he could only manage a look of disgust.

"Is he wanting something?"

The young man tried to speak but found it hard to form words.

"The black dog has bitten out his tongue, she thinks. She knows what he is here for. He is here for Yuletide trinkets."

The young man gathered his senses enough to nod weakly.

"What does he want? What takes the young man's fancy?"

The young man found the wit to speak, praising the goods that lay in abundance. He asked the old pedlar woman the cost of this and the prices of that, but she sniggered at these questions and told him not to worry.

"He must choose what he likes and she will wrap it and pack it and put it in his carriage."

So the young man pointed out the things he liked the most. She took each one in her frail old hands, wrapping each in dark brown paper before placing them safely inside a wooden crate. When the crate was full and sitting behind the driving seat, the young man reached into his pocket.

"He needs a tree," she smiled, the wrinkles around her face forming deep dry canyons. "He must have a tree. She will pick out the best, the greenest. He will keep it in its pot and it will live the whole year through and never die. He need never buy another tree and every year it shall get bigger and bigger. Every yuletide he has will be greater than the last. Carollers will visit his house first before their voices tire. His goose shall be the fattest, his fire the warmest."

The young man watched as she chose the most splendid tree of the collection, tall (but not too tall) sturdy and the perfect shape. She picked it up without a groan, carried it to his automobile and placed it next to the crate.

The young man pulled the coins from his pocket, asking her how much all of this would cost him. She looked at the pile of silver and copper in his palm. Her fingers creaked out and chose half-a-crown from the collection. He gasped and insisted she take more. She smiled, turned her head to the side and pointed at her cheek.

"All she wants is a kiss from her young man."

The young man raised his eyebrows at this, looked about for a moment, before leaning forward to place a half-hearted kiss upon her dry old skin. The old woman giggled, skipping from his side to dance into the darkness of bramble and heather.

The young man drove home in a daze. He smiled in bewilderment at the strange transaction and tingled in excitement at how magnificent his house would look with these fine decorations on display.

Once in his house he found a place for the tree. He positioned it in a corner away from the fire. One by one he began to unwrap the baubles, dangling each before his eyes before hanging them from the sturdy branches. He marvelled at how the tree had dropped so few needles as he had struggled with it into the house. It truly was a magnificent arboreal treat for the eyes and nose. A sweet smell of pine drifted through the room as he hung the exquisite paper chains across the ceiling. The baubles cast their own warm glow as he placed five candles upon the mantelpiece. He smiled as he surveyed - what could only be described as - a piece of Yuletide art.

The floor was littered with pieces of brown paper. He felt a great weariness settle in his limbs and vowed to himself that he would clear this mess the following morning. After the excitement of the day, a good rest was needed. As he started to walk to his room one of the paper chains split from its moorings and dangled down from the ceiling rose. He sighed, contemplating grabbing a chair to put the damn thing up again. After a moment he grinned, mumbled

"Tomorrow", to himself, switched off the light and shut the door.

He slept soundly that night, waking on Christmas Eve feeling full of life. He sprang from his bed, made his toilet, dressed and ran downstairs to the drawing room. As he opened the door he stopped. He looked at the floor. All of the scattered brown paper was gone. He searched about and saw that it lay, flattened out into a neat pile, in the old wooden crate. The paper chain was hanging across the room again, secure and as solid as one could hope a paper chain could be. He scratched his head, stepped from the room and shut the door. He waited a moment and opened it again. The room was the same. Tidy. The brown paper was flat, ordered and ready to use, the paper chain still hung as it should. Maybe he had been so tired in the night he had somehow tidied all of this and forgotten every detail. But, if that was the case, he would have thrown the brown paper away, as he was not a frugal minded fellow at all.

The young man shook his head. His mother was coming this evening. She was staying the night. She was coming by train from York and he had to make ready. He walked to the kitchen. He had hung the duck in his pantry, the butcher had been kind enough to pluck and gut it but he still needed to prepare the stuffing and vegetables for tomorrow's feast. He staggered in surprise at the sight that met his eyes. Standing in pans of cold water were the carrots, sprouts and potatoes. In the cool of the pantry, under the lid of the roasting dish, sat the goose, stuffed and ready to roast tomorrow morning.

He put a hand to his head and thought back over the events of yesterday. How had he managed to blank out so many details? He had not been drunk the night before, if he had then he would be feeling most unwell and there were no symptoms of over-indulgence in his head or stomach.

He spent the rest of the morning wrapping presents for his mother. After a light lunch he delivered cards to his neighbours. The elderly couple across the way invited him in for mulled wine and a slice of cake which he greatly enjoyed. At five o'clock he made his way back to the house. He ensured his mother's bed was made and her stocking hanging by the fire. He lit the fire and switched on the lights around the tree. Running over to the gramophone he took out the Christmas 78" that he had purchased in Whitby. The needle crackled on the black vinyl and an impressive orchestra swelled. The sound was much clearer than on those old Durium discs. Mother would be impressed. The fire seemed to flicker in response to the roar of the heraldic trumpets, the branches of the tree rustled slightly. The doorbell rang. A bauble fell from the tree, rolled toward the hearth, before coming to a rest in front of the fire.

The young man looked at the bauble glinting in the light of the flickering flames. He leapt to his feet and ran for the door. His mother greeted him with a warm embrace. He led her inside, took her coat and offered her the best chair by the fire. She looked around the room with approval, commenting on the decorations, the candles, the fire and the tree. The young man looked around for the bauble, to put it back, but could see no sign of it. He checked around the hearth and under the chairs but could see nothing. He glanced at the tree and was surprised to see the very bauble he was looking for dangling in its former position. He blinked and shook his head, causing his mother to enquire after his health. Snapping to his senses he walked over to the drinks table to pour her a warming glass of brandy.

They had a hearty tea of various cheeses, slices of cold smoked sausage he had bought from the local market, all washed down with several glasses of wine. She expressed delight at each new flavour and he, eager to please, poured more wine into her glass whilst piling her plate high with cheese and slices of sausage. Eventually talk turned to how splendid the new home was and how cold and lonely she was in hers.

"I'm rattling around like an almond in a pan," she moaned. "It isn't the same since you left."

The young man smiled, trying to divert her attention with more cheese, but she was now resolutely fixed to this topic.

"I never understood why you left anyway."

He spoke of his post as schoolmaster at the local school, about the new friends he had made. How he was making his way in the world. He told her she should be proud. As he said these words he noticed that her face was growing red and tears were stinging her eyes. He then did a most foolish thing. Rather than comfort and placate his mother he felt his temper rise. He railed at her for her selfishness, he shouted at her for not letting him be. How would he meet a lady and give her the grandchildren she craved if he was still tangled up in her blessed apron strings? The room seemed to fall silent at this explosion. The needle was scratching against the paper in the centre of the 78". His mother rose unsteadily from her chair, a wine glass in her hand. Her face was scarlet with rage.

"You ungrateful boy!" she screamed, throwing the glass from her. It smashed against the stone hearth, sending crystal splinters across the carpet. The young man realised he had gone too far. He ran over to his mother, holding her hand to calm her down. She sank into her chair, apologising for the glass. The air was full of remorse and regret. He told her not to concern herself with the glass. He had plenty more. He stroked her aging head and sang her a carol. When he had finished he saw that her eyes were closed. Rather than disturb her, he covered her in a blanket and stoked the fire before stuffing both of their stockings with Santa's goodies.

He crept upstairs to bed.

The fire crackled.

The branches of the tree rustled.

The young man's mother slept on.

The flames danced.

The baubles swung softly.

The young man's mother snored.

Shadows played upon the wall.

The Christmas tree began to creak.

The young man's mother smacked her lips and mumbled.

Sparks jumped onto the hearth.

The creaking grew in volume. The trunk began to thicken, to swell, to widen and expand until it was the thickness of the pot that held it. A tear began to spread from the top of the trunk to its very roots. The bark split to reveal the soft light brown of pine beneath, then this too began to split further and further apart. The trunk opened up into two halves, swinging out over the edges of the pot. Standing in the centre of the pot was a tiny wrinkled old woman. She opened her eyes, stepping from the pot onto the floor before surveying the room with a "tut-tut".

"What a mess," she muttered as she saw the 78" out of its sleeve. She picked it up, gave it a wipe and carefully put it in the box next to the gramophone stand. She looked at the glass scattered across the floor and tutted. After picking each piece up and placing them carefully in the wastepaper bin she walked back towards the tree.

A violent snore erupted from behind her. She turned to look at the young man's mother sitting in front of the fire, her eyelids flickering, and her hair a halo of static chaos around her head.

Her mouth was open, drool dripping from her lips onto the blanket. Snores erupted from her mouth like flatulent eruptions from the backend of a pig.

"What a mess," muttered the ancient crone, walking towards the chair. She looked at the mother for a moment, wincing as another unearthly snore disrupted the peace of the household. "She'll wake the whole street, she will."

The hag reached out a hand and pinched the mother's nose. A sudden snore exploded from her mouth. The hag clamped her hand over the mother's lips, causing her to open her eyes in shock. She could see this tiny ancient woman in front of her, sitting on her lap, fingers pinching her nose, hand on her mouth. She fought to breathe but could not. She struggled to pull her head away, tried to stand, pulling her hands from under the blanket to push this monstrous old crone away. No matter what she did the hag's grip was relentless, unyielding. The mother started to weaken, her limbs grew limp. She slumped. Her eyes turned to frosted glass. The crone waited a minute more before relaxing her grip. With the greatest of care she began to strip the old woman of her clothes taking off her own and replacing them with those taken from the young man's mother. That done, she lifted the woman above her head before carrying her to the open tree in the corner of the room. The hag pushed the body into the centre of the pot, placing her old rags on top of the corpse. She watched as the sides of the tree swung closed, as the tear mended, the bark reformed, the trunk shrunk back to its former shape, the baubles stopped swinging and the branches stopped rustling. The hag threw another log onto the fire, sat in the chair, covered herself in her blanket and waited for the dawn to come. As she slept her skin began to lose some of its wrinkles, she began to stretch and grow.

She did not snore.

In the morning the young man bounded down the stairs to find his mother standing at the mantelpiece, all beaming smiles, a stuffed stocking in her hands.

"He must see what Father Christmas has brought him," she said.

The Straw Pledge

(And other Yuletide larks)

There are a variety of fascinating games one can play at Yuletide. Some of the following games are suitable for the household, others for the tavern, whilst the remainder (such as the Straw Pledge) are best played when you are out and about.

These games have been collected from various sources. Sir Stanley Coulton, an essayist and poet, recorded several of these games on his journeys on the North York Moors in the late 19th century. Lord Brightwater and his team also made note of various pastimes and games in their investigations of the Black Meadow in the 1930s. The researcher Roger Mullins was particularly fond of the Straw Pledge until a series of strange and unfortunate incidents at the British Museum turned him against that particular game.

"Lumme! That's two more points for Nicholas!"

The Straw Pledge, as everyone knows, is a popular game in the villages around the Black Meadow. The main aim of the game is to put pieces of straw in people's pockets without them noticing. The rules state that you would gain one point for a friend's pocket; two points for a stranger; three points for a priest and four points for a constable.

Hence the old rhyme:

One for a friend
For a friend will not mind
That a small piece of straw
Will bless his behind.

Two for a stranger
But beware, still your hay
For a stranger may turn
To strike you away!

Three for a priest
Though the score you may swell
If he spies you behind him
He'll send you to hell!

Four for a constable
You'll scream and you'll wail
When he claps you in irons
And sends you to jail!

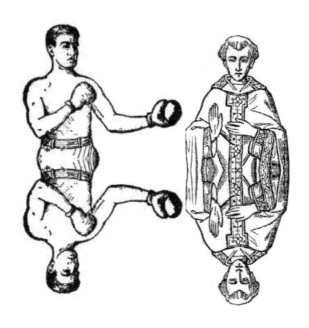

Although frowned upon by the clergy (due to its provocative title) **Punch the Vicar** was a very popular game amongst children of the Black Meadow. While it is true that people were somewhat suspicious of priests, (in many tales from the Black Meadow they are often seen as untrustworthy or corrupt), in reality relationships between the church and village were cordial and jolly. Although the name brings to mind scenes of violence against innocent men of the cloth, it is actually a devilishly simple game which rarely put anyone in physical danger.

A member of the Brightwater team made the following observations about a game he witnessed:

"Seven children were standing in a large circle. An eighth child was standing in the centre wearing a clerical collar made of paper. The child would run around the interior of the circle whilst the children (who were forbidden to move) reached out their right hands to grab at the collar. If the collar was grabbed, the victor would playfully punch the "vicar" on the arm and then don the collar themselves. And on it would repeat."

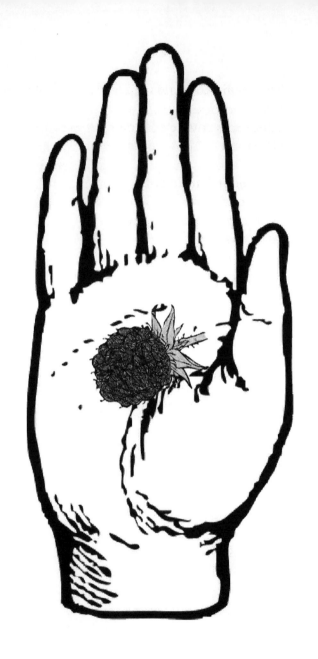

To explain the rules of **Don't squash the blackberry** the best source to use is this children's rhyme collected by Sir Stanley Coulton:

Hold your hands out
Boys and Girls
Drop down the berry black
Let it rest snug
In your palms
And wait for the attack

Slap your palms down
Boys and Girls
On your partner's berry
If they're too slow
Then let the mess
Make your soul be merry

Have you won then
Boys and Girls?
Check your sticky fingers.
If you've lost
Lick off the mess
A'while the berry lingers

Who's in the coal cellar?

This very strange game has various iterations depending on the type of people who play it. The game starts when a large group of people are invited to a house. When the very first person arrives the host locks them in the cellar. Once all the other guests have arrived and the food has been eaten the game begins. The host cries out:

"Who's in the coal cellar?"

The gathered guests try to work out who is missing from the party. The game can take a long or short time depending on how well known the missing guest is. When the missing guest is identified they are released from the cellar and given a flagon of wine and a specially prepared dish of lamb and potato stew.

If the guest remains unidentified then they remain there for the rest of the evening and leave, after all of the others have gone, under cover of darkness.

In aristocratic households the game is quite different. The lord of the manor will send out his servants to find an individual with an unusual occupation from the surrounding villages. That person will then be persuaded or coerced to come with them to the manor house where they are locked in the cellar. The game then plays out in much the same way, though with the occupation rather than the identity of the missing guest being surmised.

The missing guest is often paid for the ignominy caused by the game. If they remain unidentified they are paid double the agreed rate.

(Source: Undiscovered Heresies – Roger Mullins – published 1975.)

The Black Star

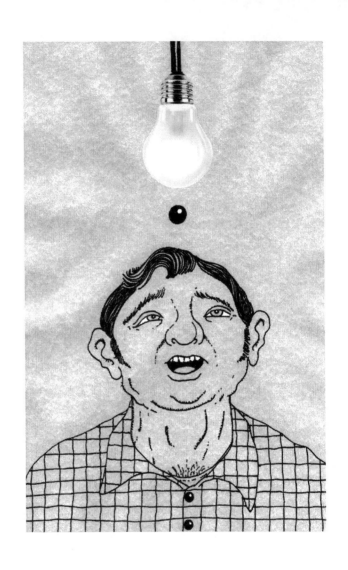

The Black Star

This story is based on the eye-witness account of an event that occurred in Christmas 1959.

It is the most recent tale collected by Roger Mullins before his disappearance in 1972. It is based on an interview that he conducted with Mr and Mrs Tresham in 1968 as well as an account by an unnamed RAF Officer who had collected various pieces of evidence about the phenomena known as "Land Spheres".

Up on the meadow the Land Sphere sat waiting. Watching the lights glinting in the town below. A shudder rippled across its intangible black hide. A tiny bulge appeared on its side like a boil on the skin of an elephant. The sphere shuddered again. The bulge became more distinct, breaking the surface. A tiny, perfect circle. Pushing out. Breaking away from the skin of the sphere. A tearing popping sound would have been heard if anyone was near. With a final pop, like a cork from a bottle, the circle left its host and floated alongside it. A tiny sphere next to its enormous parent. The Land Sphere

99

sank into the ground, leaving the tiny black circle alone, observing all the different coloured lights in the distance. It wobbled slightly in the air, seeming uncertain. Gradually it edged towards the nearest light emanating from a cottage on the edge of the meadow. As the light grew more distinct, so the tiny black sphere picked up its pace, until, before long, it sat in the air just outside the window of Farmer Tresham's cottage.

Mr and Mrs Tresham were sitting examining the new lights on the Christmas tree. Mr Tresham was telling his wife how his own father used to put candles on the tree and of how his house had nearly caught fire in the Christmas of 1909. His wife smiled, telling him that she had heard this tale before. She did admit however that the new multi-coloured lights were very special and added a certain something to the house. She expected that their grandchildren would be very excited by the tree and its splendid lights.

There was a knock at the window. Mr Tresham frowned.
"Who could that be at this hour and in this weather?"

Mrs Tresham looked out of the window, but could see nothing.

"Perhaps it was just the wind," she said.

"Perhaps," her husband agreed.

There was another knock.

"It could be a bird flying into the window," she said, peering out.

Again a knock.

"Or a bat?"

"They know where they're going," her husband laughed.

Another knock.

"Right, that's enough," said Mr Tresham, making for the front door. "Some 'orrid little blighter outside chucking gravel, I shouldn't wonder."

As he pulled the door open he felt a slight breeze as though something tiny was flying past him. Mr Tresham looked outside. Seeing nothing he yelled a warning into the dark.

"I know you're out there. You knock it off right now, or I'll call the police and get onto your parents!"

He pulled the door shut, slowly scrutinising the darkened yard as he did so.

"Didn't see anyone," he shrugged.

Mrs Tresham was surprisingly silent. He turned to face his wife and found that she had her back to him. She seemed to be staring intently at something in the centre of the room. He stepped forward to see a small black ball floating just beneath the light bulb hanging down from the ceiling.

"What is that?" he managed.

Mrs Tresham shushed him and they gazed at the little black sphere in wonder. It floated up towards the glowing bulb, touching the glass briefly. As it made contact, the bulb seemed to darken for a moment, the sphere wobbled in the air, vibrating suddenly and viciously. After a moment it became still and dropped to the floor, lying immobile and lifeless.

"Have you ever seen the like before?" Mrs Tresham wondered.

Mr Tresham shook his head and edged forward. He touched the sphere with the edge of his foot and found that he could not move it. His wife joined him and they both crouched down to study the intruder.

"It's perfectly black."

"What is it?"

"Looks like a marble."

He tried to pick it up but found that it was stuck fast to the boards.

Mrs Tresham bit her lip. "I don't like it," she said.

She walked over to the sideboard, pulled a glass bowl from the bottom shelf, before placing it upside down over the little black sphere.

They stood for a while gazing at the ball. After some time had passed and it appeared to be utterly still, they went about their chores. Mr Tresham finished hanging up the baubles, ensuring that each was placed in such a way as to reflect the beautiful new lights.

He switched off the main light so only the tree lights were illuminating the room. As soon as he did so the bowl on the floor began to rattle. Mr Tresham immediately turned on the main light. The bowl instantly became silent. The sphere sat on the boards as it had a moment ago. Mr Tresham raised an eyebrow.

He switched off the light again.

The bowl rattled.

He turned it on.

The bowl was still.

He switched it off.

Rattle.

On.

Silence.

Off.

Rattle.

On.

Silence.

He paused, his curiosity building. He turned the light off. As the bowl began to rattle and shake he walked over to it, trying to discern what was happening beneath the glass. He could make out, in the dim multi-coloured light, the ball pushing against the curve of the glass. The bowl scraped slightly against the floorboards, moving an inch towards the lights. Gradually, with little rattling jumps, the bowl moved closer, inch by inch, to the Christmas tree. When it reached the edge of the rug, it stopped, unable to move any further. The ball began to move more frantically back and forth, throwing itself against the glass, trying in vain to get the bowl to move over the raised edge of the rug.

"Everything all right out there?" Mrs Tresham called from the kitchen. Mr Tresham switched the main light on, causing the rattling to stop.
"Everything's fine," he shouted back.
Tiptoeing towards the bowl, a boyish curiosity rose in his gullet. He lifted the glass, placed it to one side, exposing the black sphere to the air. He walked back to the light switch, watching the ball intently as he did so.

His hand hovered over the switch. Glancing nervously at the door of the kitchen he pressed it down.

Instantly the ball shot into the air. It flew with astonishing speed towards the tree. Mr Tresham switched the light back on. The ball stopped. Stock still in mid-air. Hovering, waiting, unsure. Filled with resolve and scientific zeal, Mr Tresham turned the main light off. The ball sped to the tree, halting by a blue light. The black sphere touched the light source, became transparent for a moment, then blue, then black again. The light from the bulb was gone, though the other lights still shone brightly, which struck Mr Tresham as strange. The ball moved to a red bulb, swallowing its light. To a green, a yellow, a purple, a red, a blue, all around the tree, over and over and over. Sometimes it would fly to a bauble, touch the reflection until it faded before attacking the bulb next to it. Soon the tree sat in darkness. The only light from the room came from the fire blazing in the grate. The little ball flew from the tree to the fireplace. The flames grew dimmer and dimmer, they did not flicker and extinguish, instead their colour and light faded away. Putting his hand out, Mr

Tresham could still feel the intense heat from the invisible flames. The ball was lighter in shade now.

The kitchen door creaked open. Mr Tresham ran to the switch, turning on the main light. The ball was hidden in the black flames of the fire.

"What's happened to the lights?" Mrs Tresham asked, looking at the tree.

"Dodgy wiring I think. I'll take them back."

"Why's the fire gone out? I'm sure I just put a couple of logs on it a few minutes ago. Did you spill something on it?"

Mrs Tresham walked over to the fireplace, putting her hand into the heart of a black flame. She cried out as intense pain flared in her hand. Her skin crackled, flamed, charred. Mr Tresham pulled her away in an instant, led her quickly to the kitchen, where he placed her hand in a basin of cold water, running the tap constantly.

"Don't move."

Mr Tresham pulled up a tall stool, sitting his quivering wife down next to the sink. She sobbed at the pain. He ran to the cupboard to find two aspirin, which he fed to her. He stood with her until her shaking subsided, stroking her hair, whispering words of calm. Soon her hand grew numb.

"What happened to the flame?"

Mr Tresham looked shamefaced. He told her of the sphere's adventures. Of how it was still when the room was bathed in light but how it came to life when it was dark and it sought out and found the little light sources. How it would swallow the lights.

"Swallow the lights?" she said. "Are they still on, like the flame?"

"I think so."

"Have you tried turning them off and on again?"

Mr Tresham shook his head. He was pleased that his wife had the same curiosity as him and cursed himself for not sharing his discoveries sooner.

He wedged the kitchen door open so that his wife could see the tree. He switched the lights off, turned them on, astonished to see the lights return to their former glory.

"Watch," he said to his wife, walking over the main light to switch it off. The black sphere darted from the fire to the tree, gobbling voraciously at the lights. Once finished it flew into the kitchen where it wavered uncertainly in the bright glow.

Mr Tresham flicked the Christmas lights off and on. The tree lights flickered into life again but the sphere stayed floating a few feet from Mrs Tresham.

"Take it to Peter Sykes," she said suddenly.

"The science teacher?"

"He'll know what it is."

"Will he?"

"He'll know more than us."

Mr Tresham grabbed the glass bowl and the plate. He placed the bowl over the floating sphere before putting the plate underneath trapping it inside. As he moved the bowl he felt considerable resistance as the sphere tried to maintain its position in mid-air. It pressed itself against the glass. Mr Tresham found the going tough, having to drag the glass bowl down to a lower and more comfortable height to carry. He pulled and pushed the bowl from the house to the car, looking like a mime artist fighting with an immovable balloon.

After checking on his wife and assuring her that he would bring a doctor back with him (though she told him not to worry) he drove into town. As he drew closer to the Christmas lights adorning the shop windows of Malton the sphere began to rattle excitedly inside its glass cage. It became more violent as he stepped out of the car to visit the public house that Peter Sykes was known to frequent. He found himself shushing and speaking calming words to the little ball. It appeared to respond, albeit briefly, for, as soon as he rounded the corner into the main marketplace and saw all of the lights hanging across the street, with the bright multi-coloured displays in the windows, the ball took to making such a frenzied attempt to escape that Mr Tresham lost his grip of the plate and bowl momentarily. The bowl and plate smashed on the ground causing the little black sphere to fly wild and free. It darted from light to light, sucking up the delicious brightness, leaving each light dead and dark. The speed of its movement was astonishing.

People out window-shopping looked up in wonder. They could not make out the ball, but they could see light after light turning out, spreading from display to display, decoration to decoration. They also noticed a strange man following the devastation whistling and calling;

"Come by. Stop that now. That's enough. Back you come. Come by, that's a good lad. Come on. You've had your fill. That'll do."

They whispered to each other. Wasn't that Mr Tresham from up the hill? Had he taken leave of his senses? Mr Tresham was oblivious to their gossiping, he was desperate to stop the little sphere from doing any extra damage. But it was no good. Before long all the lights in the street were dark and people could make out a little glowing multi-coloured sphere buzzing above their heads, moving from shop to shop, street to street, faster and faster and faster. Consuming the light from artificial stars, neon Santas, lights around trees and windows. In and out of gaps in windows, gaps under doors. People began to chase, desperate to stamp it beneath their feet, to catch it between their hands. Mr Tresham found an old tin bucket and began banging it with a stick.

"Come on little fella. You must be full up now. You must be full. Time to go home."

He found that the chase had brought him outside the pub he had been looking for. The lights were out and the customers had spilled out onto the pavement. They were watching the progress of the sphere with interest and awe. Keeping half an eye on the devastation being wrought, Mr Tresham found Peter Sykes, pipe clamped between his teeth, eyes fixed on the sphere as it flew from street lamp to street lamp. The ball was brighter now and slightly larger.

"What do you make of that, Mr Sykes?" he asked.

"Seems to like the lights, doesn't it?" the teacher mused, a cloud of tobacco smoke framing his face.

The crowd watched as one by one all of the Christmas lights of Malton winked out until the light of the star on the town tree was the only source of artificial illumination.

Mr Tresham could see the ball as it absorbed the final light from the Christmas star from the top of the tree. The star turned black. The light of the moon seemed brighter now that the town was in darkness. The sphere hovered by the black star. Mr Tresham ran down the high street banging his bucket frantically.

"Come on! Back you come! I'll take you home."

The sphere waited for a moment, hovering uncertainly. It flew down to Mr Tresham, floating a few inches from his face.

"Come on boy," he pleaded. "Back in the bucket. Where it's safe."

The sphere wobbled in the air, gave a little shudder and a tiny buzz. Without warning it shot up vertically, higher and higher towards the moon.

"No! You can't have that! It's too big for you little fella!"

By now the black ball was a tiny speck of dust against the round expanse of the shining moon. Mr Tresham felt a great wave of sadness overwhelm him.

"Come back," he croaked. "Come back. You can have all the Christmas lights that you can eat."

He turned to the crowd "We can turn them back on, just switch them off and on again. The lights will come back. I've seen it happen."

But the crowd weren't listening. They were all looking up, a vast shadow passing over their moonlit faces. Mr Tresham followed their gaze. The moon was slowly disappearing, an enormous black sphere was moving, obscuring its light, blocking a quarter, a half, three quarters. The little multi-coloured shining ball sped towards the side of this monstrous circle. It drew close to the skin of the enormous dark sphere. The membranes of the smaller and larger sphere touched, joining, the light fading. The little ball forming part of its surface, becoming a lump, then a blemish before vanishing within the body of the giant. The vast sphere began to move away, unblocking the light of the moon. It moved further and further away, disappearing into the distant winter mists.

The lights of the town started to flicker into life. Mr Tresham stood, feeling a strange sensation of regret and loss that he knew was utterly inexplicable and unnecessary. He sniffed and wiped his eyes.

At home once the doctor had left, Mrs Tresham found her husband painting one of his golf balls in the lounge.
"Black, husband?"
"My little black star," he said. "I know I'll never see the like again."

So Mrs Tresham, hand bandaged, helped her husband attach some wire to the ball, before placing it on top of the tree.

If you are ever fortunate enough to visit the Tresham household at Christmas time ask them about the Black Star. Mr Tresham will tell you, eyes glistening, that one day he hopes to see their tiny visitor again.

About the Author

Chris Lambert – Storyteller – Teacher – Traveller of Mist – Mythogeographer – Demiurge - Liar

Chris Lambert is the curator of the Black Meadow and its associated phenomena. He works closely with Kev Oyston as part of "The Soulless Party" to uncover the mysteries hidden within its dense mist.

He writes far too much. As well as the critically lauded Tales from the Black Meadow and Songs from the Black Meadow he has also had short stories published in The Ghastling, The Dead Files and Tales of the Damned. He has had four plays published and over 20 performed professionally including: The Simple Process of Alchemy, Loving Chopin and Ship of Fools. He occasionally dabbles with music too.

For more of Lambert visit:
Blackmeadowtales.blogspot.co.uk
Musicforzombies.blogspot.co.uk
Lambertthewriter.blogspot.co.uk

About the Illustrators

Nigel Wilson is an artist, singer, actor and prop-maker.

He illustrated "Tales from the Black Meadow" and "Some Words with a Mummy". He plays a fantastic Father Christmas and has a beautiful bass singing voice.

Andy Paciorek is a graphic artist and writer, drawn mainly to the worlds of myth, folklore, symbolism, decadence, curiosa, anomaly, dark romanticism and otherworldly experience. He is fascinated both by the beautiful and the grotesque and the twilight threshold consciousness where these boundaries blur. The mist-gates, edges and liminal zones where nature borders supernature and daydreams and nightmares cross paths are of great inspiration.

He has worked for various clients and outlets including Harper Collins, Cumbrian Cthulhu and Wyrd Harvest Press.

He is also the creator of the Folk Horror Revival project.

"The stand out entries include "Beyond the Moor" a poem about a maiden accosted by a bandit who remains unafraid due to having been to the "beyond" of the title and returned. Also of note are "Children of the Black Meadow" where a bereaved mother resurrects her deceased kids as blackberry bramble homunculi; cyclical damnation tale "The Coal Man and the Creature" and the paranoia-inducing sucker punch "The Watcher From the Village" ... this is a collection that strongly invites a second reading.." - STARBURST MAGAZINE

"A banquet of weirdness..." – Hypnobobs

"...visceral dread slowly rises from its mustiness..." – Mythogeography

"A fine piece of British Hauntology" - Gareth Rees Author of Marshland

When Professor R. Mullins of the University of York went missing in 1972 on the site of the area known as Black Meadow atop of the North Yorkshire Moors, he left behind him an extensive body of work that provided a great insight into the folklore of this mysterious place. Writer Chris Lambert has been rooting through Mullins' files for over ten years and now presents this collection of weird and macabre tales.

Marvel at tales such as The Rag and Bone Man, The Meadow Hag, The Fog House, The Land Spheres and The Children of the Black Meadow.

What is the mystery surrounding The Coalman and the Creature?

Who or what is The Watcher in the Village?

What is the significance of the Shining Apples?

Why is it dangerous to watch the Horsemen dance?

Beautifully illustrated by Nigel Wilson these tales will haunt you for a long time to come.

Exiled Publications – Available from Amazon

"Tales From the Black Meadow takes this idea one step further, providing an actual CD of music to accompany the stories. All but one track is named after one of the tales and the music of each complements its narrative counterpart. The slight scratchy crackle of the music effectively dates it, making it sound as though it could have been copied from a vinyl record from the '70s. ... atmospheric precision..."
Andrew Marshall - Starburst Magazine

"Listen to Tales From The Black Meadow and be introduced to the strange and wonderful world of Hammer Horror, of British Folklore, of Radiophonic Scores and things that go bump in the night. A delirious and delicious mystery..." Forest Punk

"An irresistibly evocative title that no budding hauntologist could rightly ignore.." The Active Listener

"To me, it easily sounds like the opening to a television show from the late 70's. I can see the title card and the credits appearing over gently revolving images...One

122

could still listen to the record and have a sense of the supernatural and the uncanny; dark foggy nights can be heard in the muted tracks. Little details give the songs on Tales from the Black Meadow their spooky spice, such as the soft crackling on each track, giving it the feel of an old vinyl record..." Fascination with Fear

"Tales From The Black Meadow is one of the best releases we had this year, with ten marvellous compositions to state it.." Music Blob (Blog)

"If you enjoy a bit of Folklore, Poetry, A Mystery on the moors, 1970s kids TV and some very lovely haunting music, then this book and CD are an absolute must.." Keith Seatman - Test Transmission

Professor R. Mullins, a classics professor, had a great interest in Black Meadow, in particular its folklore and spent many years documenting its history and tales that were part of the local oral tradition. In his office, his colleagues found over twenty thick notebooks crammed with stories and interviews from the villages around Black Meadow.

Some of these stories seemed to be from the legendary disappearing village itself and provided some vital clues as to how the phenomena was interpreted and explained by the local populace.

In 1978, Radio 4 produced a now rare documentary about the folklore, mystery and tales surrounding the Black Meadow area. It also featured music specially commissioned to accompany the programme. This music has recently been unearthed by the Mullins Estate and carefully isolated for your listening pleasure.

These stories, poems and songs have also been gathered together to capture the unsettling nature of the Black Meadow.

Do not listen to this on your own at night and make sure you shut your windows. Listen for the stamping feet of the horsemen, avoid the gaze of the Watcher in the village and do not walk into the mist.

Available to buy from Bandcamp

123

17 Musical Artists from around the world
15 tracks
All inspired by "Tales from the Black Meadow"

Featuring music by:

Hare and the Moon and Alison O'Donnell - Lost Trail - Wyrdstone
The Rowan Amber Mill and Angeline Morrison - The Implicit Order
Emily Jones - Elena Martin - Eastgreen - Keith Seatman - The Soulless Party
Mervyn Williams and the Theale Green Senior Choir - Winterberry
Septimus Keen - Kid Moxie - Joseph Curwen

Mastered by Chris "concretism" Sharp
Produced by Chris Lambert for Exiled
CD illustrated by Nigel Wilson

Released by Mega Dodo
All profits go to Cancer Research UK
www.mega-dodo.co.uk

A book is also available from Amazon

"Songs From The Black Meadow is a deeply involving and atmospherically congruent undertaking, swathed in the beckoning hauntology of the fictitious-or-is-it Black Meadow itself." - **Record Collector**

"The breadth of artists who have opted to contribute to this new collection of songs inspired by Chris Lambert's book of short stories "Tales from the Black Meadow" is a testament to the universal appeal that Lambert's stories have managed to draw..." - **The Active Listener**

"Sometimes frivolous, sometimes chilling, let this be your entrance into one of modern acid folk's most pervasive myths." – **Goldmine Magazine**

"...a fine collection of psychedelic folk and goth tinged songs... the sense of mystery and journey is present here and this a great pleasure to listen to." – **DC Rock Live**

"The Black Meadow is a place in people's psyche – the fact this compilation gently stresses over and over again. Here's a legend for a new kind of perception." – **House of Prog**

"Songs From The Black Meadow is a well-realized, immersive concept that will pull you in, and never let you go. It serves as an additional soundtrack for some damn fine horrors, and also stands alone as a weird, supernatural journey all its own." – **Forestpunk**

125

Strange Lands by Andrew Paciorek is a deeply researched and richly illustrated information guide to the entities and beasts of Celtic myth & legend and to the many strange beings that have entered the lore of the land through the influence of other cultures and technological evolution.

At nearly 400 pages and featuring over 170 original illustrations, Strange Lands is an essential accompaniment for both the novice and seasoned walkers between worlds.

Available from Blurb

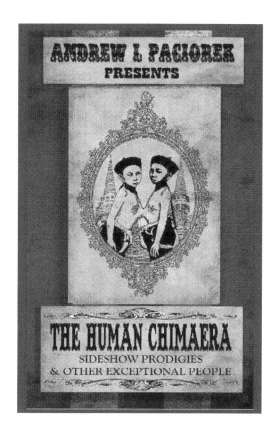

The Human Chimaera
Andrew Paciorek
Containing over 100 original pen & ink portraits
alongside biographic text, The Human Chimaera
is an indispensable guide to the greatest stars of
the circus sideshows and dime museums.
Includes a foreword by John Robinson of
Sideshow World.

Available from Blurb

Folk Horror Revival: Corpse Roads
An epic collection of spellbinding poetry,
focusing on folk horror, life, death and the
eeriness of the landscape by many creative
talents both living and departed. Accompanied
throughout with atmospheric imagery by an
impressive collection of contemporary
photographers.

Wyrd Harvest Press

Folk Horror Revival: Field Studies

Featuring essays and interviews by many great cinematic, musical, artistic and literary talents, Folk Horror Revival: Field Studies is the most comprehensive and engaging exploration to date of the sub genre of Folk Horror and associated fields in cinema, television, music, art, culture and folklore. Includes contributions by Kim Newman, Robin Hardy, Thomas Ligotti, Philip Pullman, Gary Lachman and many many more.

Wyrd Harvest Press

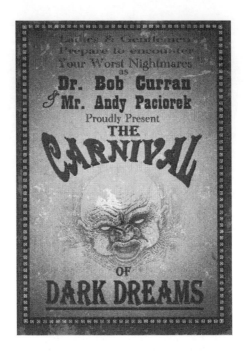

The Carnival of Dark Dreams
Dr Bob Curran & Andy Paciorek

Welcome to The Carnival of Dark Dreams. A visual daytrip into the depths of the jungle, the sands of the desert, to many haunted habitats and worse still into the darkness of the human imagination. But fear not, for captured, caged and presented for your curiosity by Dr. Bob Curran and Mr. Andy Paciorek are some of the most deadly, grotesque, fearsome entities of world folklore. Roll up Roll up for the fright of your lives. Dare you visit The Carnival of Dark Dreams?

Wyrd Harvest Press

Printed in Great Britain
by Amazon